TRACTOR

SALLY SUTTON · ILLUSTRATED BY BRIAN LOVELOCK

WALKER BOOKS
AND SUBSIDIARIES
LONDON • BOSTON • SYDNEY • AUCKLAND

Down on the farm, let's cut the earth.

Chop, chop! Don't stop!

Break that ground!

Down on the farm, let's cut the earth.

What makes that cut-cut-cutting sound?

This Walker book belongs to:

For Grayson and Evan — S.S.

In memory of my father, a Kiwi farmer — B.L.

First published 2022

This edition published by Walker Books Ltd
87 Vauxhall Walk, London SE11 5HJ

10 9 8 7 6 5 4 3 2 1

This book has been typeset in Bauer Grotesk

Printed in China

British Library Cataloguing in Publication Data: a catalogue record for this book is available from the British Library

ISBN 978-1-5295-0249-7

www.walker.co.uk

It's a plough!

Down on the farm, let's till the soil.

Turn it! Churn it!

Bye-bye, weeds!

Down on the farm, let's till the soil.

What makes it nice for planting seeds?

It’s a harrow!

Down on the farm, let's plant the seeds.

Tip them! Flip them!

Go, go, go!

Down on the farm, let's plant the seeds.

What gets them set to grow, grow, grow?

It’s a seed drill!

Down on the farm, let's squirt the dirt.

Whoosh it! Swoosh it!

Splish! Splash! Spray!

Down on the farm, let's squirt the dirt.

What's watering those fields today?

It’s a sprinkler!

Down on the farm, let's reap the crop.

Rake it! Shake it!

Click! Clack! Click!

Down on the farm, let's reap the crop.

What makes the harvest super quick?

It's a combine harvester!

Down on the farm, let's move the corn.

Shift it! Lift it!

Hit the road!

Down on the farm, let's move the corn.

What brings the truck its yummy load?

It's a dump cart!

Down on the farm, let's take a break.

Munch it! Crunch it!
Taste the crop!

Down on the farm, let's take a break.

What's worked so hard it needs to stop?

It's our TRACTOR!

PARTS OF A TRACTOR

A tractor is a strong vehicle used on a farm for pulling, lifting, and powering heavy machinery.

Steering wheel: The steering wheel turns the tractor's front wheels.

Engine: A strong engine makes the wheels go around and helps the tractor to pull heavy loads.

Wheels: The front wheels steer the tractor. The large back wheels make the tractor go. The thick rubber tread provides a strong grip on the ground.

Roll bar: A roll bar protects the driver if the tractor tips over. Most large tractors now have a safety cabin that the driver sits in to protect them.

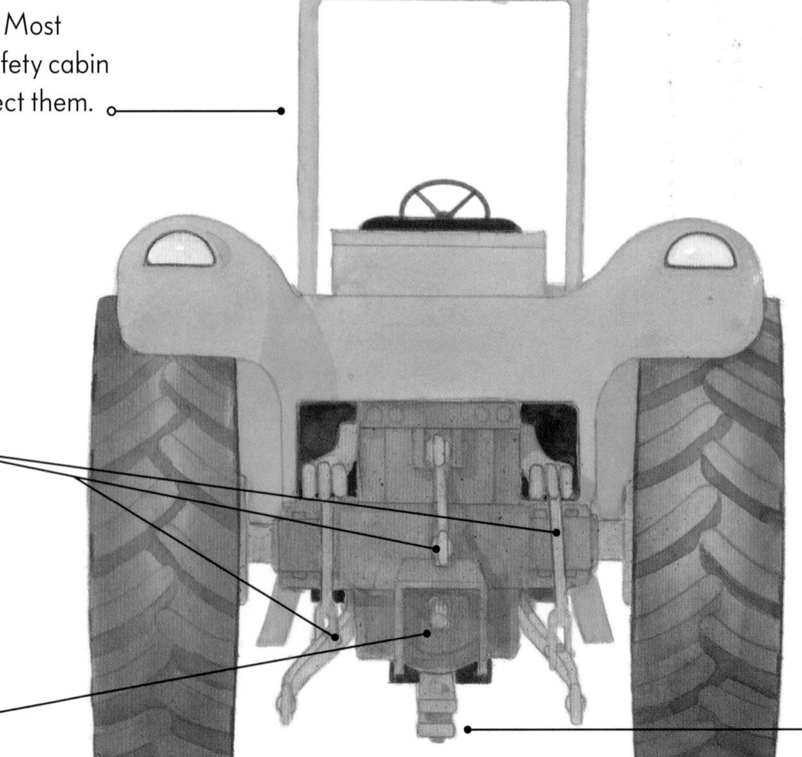

Three-point linkage: The three-point linkage, which includes the two lifting arms, attaches equipment to the tractor and keeps it secure.

Power take-off (PTO): When the rotating shaft turns, it powers the other machines connected to the tractor, such as a mower, hay baler or harvester.

Drawbar: The drawbar is used for pulling machines.